My Fingerpaint Masterpiece

by

Sherrill S. Cannon

Illustrations by Kalpart

Strategic Book Publishing and Rights Co.

Strategic Book Publishing and Rights Co.
12620 FM 1960, Suite A4-507
Houston, TX 77065
www.sbpra.com

ISBN: 978-1-62857-288-9

For my sons
Kell and KC
My Masterpieces!

As always, for the grands…
Chloe
Colby
Cristian
Josh
Kelsey
Kylie
Lindsay
Mikaila
Parker
Tucker

Also…
Kudos to KJ & her team of artists at Kalpart
who have illustrated this "Masterpiece"

One day in my art class,
Ms. Gallagher said,

"Just fingerpaint something
you see in your head."

So I dipped all my fingers
in paint that was green

And drew on the paper
my very best scene.

Then right in the middle, I put a red blob

'Cause I wasn't quite sure how to best
draw my dog;

But then the bell rang,
so I put things away

And never got back to my picture
that day.

When time to go home came, I put on my coat

And put on my hat, packed my things in my tote;

And carefully holding my fingerpaint print,

Walked out of the building and into the wind.

It was blowing and gusting, it looked like a storm.

I hoped that my jacket would help me stay warm.

I reached for my hat and I helped it to stay,

Then realized my picture was blowing away!

That wind took my picture up high in the sky,

It tossed it and turned it and helped it to fly!

The Rainbow Connection

It flew down the block and right up to the door

Of The Rainbow Connection: the art dealer's store.

I saw where it landed, it caused me to smile.

My picture was part of the artist's new pile!

He was sorting through prints for his upcoming show,

Choosing which ones would stay and which ones would go.

I don't think he saw it, he never did stop;

When my picture landed, he put one on top.

Then gathered them up with my picture inside,

And handed the pile to the dealer with pride.

I thought to myself, *It's too hard to explain,*

I'd better get home before it starts to rain.

I knew they'd find out that they'd made a mistake,

They'd know that my picture was really a fake;

For it's not by an artist, and really quite boring.

By the time I got home, it was really pouring!

My mother was mad, for I'd gotten quite wet

And broken the rules she and father had set:

That no matter what happened I'd walk straight on home,

And never go anywhere else all alone.

All thoughts of my print went right out of my head

As she fed me my dinner and sent me to bed.

Imagine my wonder when later that week,

When my mother and I went to buy me some sneaks,

An artists' display was set up in the mall

And there was my print, hanging up on the wall!!!!

It was beautifully matted and had a wood frame.

When I looked in its corner, I could see no name.

I knew that they'd never believe it was mine,

Sadly my name I'd forgotten to sign.

(My teacher had told me to sign
my own name

On all of my work, so I knew whom
to blame.)

The judges were looking at all on display.

The exhibit was very important that day,

For all of the artists were hoping to win

The grand prize blue ribbon and a chance to break in:

To become an artist of greatest renown

And be famous and honored throughout the town.

The judges stopped finally in front of my print

And studied it open-eyed, then with a squint.

They looked at it smiling, and then with a frown;

One looked at it side-ways, and one upside down!

I don't think they really knew just what it was.

Even I, though I drew it, wasn't certain because

It wasn't quite finished: my dog was a blob,

And I wished that I'd made sure to finish the job!

Embarrassed and blushing, I thought they would laugh:

My dog looked much more like a big red giraffe.

The front yard I'd painted in shades of bright green

Looked like vines in a jungle in Africa scene!

If I couldn't tell what it was, how could they?

Perhaps they would just pass it by, go away.

One judge was nodding and shaking her head,

"This print is outstanding! I want it!!" she said.

"I love it," said another; "It's great!!" said one man,

"Soon all of the world will be this artist's fan!

The color and depth of this beautiful scene

Sets a standard of excellence I've never seen!"

Said the head judge, while holding the ribbon of blue,

"Its texture and brush strokes are something brand new,

Its deep inner meaning is really quite clear.

I award it first place!" and the crowd gave a cheer.

And suddenly everyone started to try

To explain what they saw in my picture, while I

Just stood there, amazed at what I saw and heard.

"It's the sun in the sky", "No, it's really a bird!"

"It must be a flower," "I think it's a frog!"

I thought to myself, *No, it's really my dog.*

Disgusted, I finally let out a shout,

"It's my print that you all are raving about!"

"I painted that picture in art class at school.

I'm really quite sorry I had you all fooled.

The wind took it from me and blew it away

And into the Rainbow Connection one day."

The judges just stared at me, rolling their eyes.

Said one, "You'll do anything to get that prize."

The rest just ignored me. One said with a sneer,

"You're only a child telling stories, I fear."

My mother and father just said we should leave,

For there really was no way to make them believe.

I said to my parents, "Why can't they admit

That they really don't like my print one little bit?

They don't understand it, but think that they should;

So they nod their heads wisely, pretend that it's good!

We like my painting and so do the kids,

But my print should be hanging at home on our fridge.

They think a real artist hung it in the show!!"

And if ever you need me to prove
this is so,

Just come to my town and you know
what you'll see?

My masterpiece print in the art
gallery!!!

Museum Art Gallery

Acknowledgements

Thank you as always to my publisher SBPRA - especially Robert, Kait and Lynn

And also to Ellen, Denise, Suzann, Felicia, Kim, Lee, and Roger

Special thanks to my Junior Reviewers: Addie, Alexandra, Brenna and Cassandra

Love and Hugs to Alyssa, Daisy, Jordy, Katie, Matthew, and Maya – as well as Eldon and Tristan - and Alaina and Ashlyn too!

With gratitude to those who continue to help me share my books with others:

Shari, Tertia, Donna, Barbara, Rosalie, Amy, Julian, and Pat

Thanks to my family: Kim, Cailin, Paulo, Kerry, John, Kell, Steph, KC, Christy, Megan

A Special Note from Sherrill:

Can you find my other covers in this book?

(*Peter and the Whimper-Whineys*, *The Magic Word*, *Gimme-Jimmy*, and *Manner-Man*)

Do you recognize any of the children from my other books in the scenes?

Can you find the red-dog, giraffe, bird, flower, frog and sun in the Masterpiece?

(Hint – Look at upside-down version also!)

Is the child telling the story a boy or a girl? Why do you think so?

Do you remember to put your name on your work?

Do you think the Masterpiece should have won First Place? Why?

All of Sherrill S. Cannon's books are available at http://sbpra.com/curejm where 50% of the cost of the books goes to the CureJM Foundation to help find a cure for Juvenile Myositis, an incurable children's disease. Let's find a cure!

Please consider these other award winning books by Sherrill S. Cannon:

Manner-Man is a 2013 Readers Favorite Silver Medal winner as well as a Pinnacle Achievement Award Winner, and a London Book Fair H.M.

Manner-Man is a Superhero who helps children cope with bullies, and teaches them how to look within themselves for their own superhero.

ISBN 978-1-62212-478-7 - $12.50

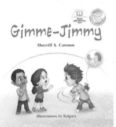

Winner of five awards: the 2013 Global eBook Silver Medal, Indie Excellence Finalist and Reader Views Finalist Awards as well as the 2012 Readers Favorite Silver Medal Award and the 2012 Pinnacle Achievement Winner Award

Gimme-Jimmy is about how a bully learns to share. His "New Polite Rule" helps him learn to make friends.

ISBN 978-1-61897-267-5 - $13.00

Winner of six awards: the 2011 Readers Favorite Gold Medal, 2011 Pinnacle Achievement Award Winner, 2011 Global Finalist Award, 2012 Reader Views Second Place, 2012 International Book Awards Finalist, and 2012 Next Generation Indie Finalist.

Elisabeth needs to learn *The Magic Word* "please", and to use it every day. Please and Thank you are words that everyone needs to use!

ISBN 978-1-6096-909-3 - $12.50

Winner of the 2011 Readers Favorite Bronze Medal and the 2011 USA Best Books Finalist Award

Peter and the Whimper-Whineys helps parents cope with whining, disguised as a fun story. Peter is a rabbit who whines all the time, and might have to join the Whimper-Whineys.

ISBN 978-1-60911-517-3 - **$13.00**

Winner of the 2011 Readers Favorite Silver Award and the 2011 Indie Excellence Finalist Award.

Santa's Birthday Gift includes Santa in the Christmas story.

(After reading a story of the nativity to my granddaughter, she asked

"But where's Santa?")

ISBN 978-1-60860-824-9 - $11.50

CPSIA information can be obtained
at www.ICGtesting.com
Printed in the USA
BVHW060346200619
551414BV00007BA/101/P